BEANIE
AND HIS DOG

by Ruth and Latrobe Carroll

Cover illustration by Nada Serafimovic and Ruth Carroll

Cover design by Elle Staples

First published in 1954

Originally titled *Tough Enough*

This unabridged version has updated grammar and spelling.

© 2019 Jenny Phillips

www.thegoodandthebeautiful.com

To
Miss Margaret Hamilton Ligon, Head of Asheville
Libraries, Asheville, North Carolina.

Mrs. Bessie Ralston, Children's Librarian, Pack
Memorial Public Library,
Asheville, North Carolina.

Miss Margaret Johnston, Librarian, Haywood
County Public Library,
Waynesville, North Carolina

Table of Contents

Chapter One 1

Chapter Two 28

Chapter Three 52

Chapter One

Beanie Tatum lived on a farm high in the Great Smoky Mountains. He had three toys of his very own, but he couldn't play with any of them. His red express wagon had a broken wheel. The broad rubber band on his slingshot had split in two. And he couldn't play

with a waterwheel his grandfather had whittled out for him, because Tatum Creek was frozen.

But he did have something alive to play with, something of his very own. It was a puppy named Tough Enough.

All the Tatums loved Tough Enough, at first. "Good dog, good dog, good dog," they said to him. He wanted to be very close to them. He lay on laps and warmed them up because, then, they warmed him up.

If he liked anybody, and he liked everybody, he licked him. He used to like the Tatums, especially Beanie. He loved Beanie best of all.

He seemed always to be hungry. When he ate, he ate fast and made small gulpy noises. Pa Tatum used to watch him and listen to him. He would laugh and slap his leg and say, "That's the *eatinest* dog!"

Tough Enough was very small, but he grew just a little every day. And the older and stronger he grew, the faster he got around and the bigger ideas he had. Some of the things he thought of to do were very bad things to do.

He was so little and so quick that, half the time, the Tatums didn't see what he was up to until he had done something bad and was ready to do something else. So some of the Tatums started not to love him so much.

Ma Tatum loved him until the time he got into the bookmobile. This was a truck with shelves built into its sides. Rows and rows and rows of books stood on those shelves.

Once, every three weeks, the bookmobile would go pushing up the road toward the Tatum farm. The Tatums and other mountain people would borrow books and keep them till the next time the bookmobile came. So it was really a little library on wheels.

A librarian drove it, and she also kept track of the books. The mountain people called her the book lady. She always brought her lunch in a cardboard box.

One time, Tough Enough sniffed out her lunch. He grabbed it. He ran off with it. He tore a hole in the box, and he ate up a chicken sandwich, a jelly sandwich, a cupcake, and a hard-boiled egg.

Ma Tatum looked very sad. She went into the kitchen. She cooked the librarian some cabbage with fatback ham and fried apples. She said she had never *ever* felt so mortified. So she didn't love Tough Enough so much. "Bad dog!" she said to him.

Buck, the oldest Tatum boy, loved Tough Enough until the morning he had trouble in the forest. He was bringing out some logs to be chopped into stove wood. He had them piled on a sled. Pal, the Tatum's horse, was pulling it.

Tough Enough ran after Pal and barked and barked and barked at his heels. Pal began to gallop. Buck couldn't manage him at all.

Pretty soon Pal slewed the sled into a stump. It turned over and spilled out the logs.

Buck had to unhook Pal's harness. He had to straighten out the reins and set the sled back on its runners. He had to lift the logs back and hitch up Pal again.

So Buck didn't love Tough Enough so much. And neither did Pal, the horse.

Serena, the oldest Tatum girl, loved Tough Enough until, one day, she hung out a big wash on a line. Tough Enough liked to chew things. He grabbed a leg of some overalls hanging on the line. He pulled.

Down came the overalls. Tough Enough growled a lot of happy little growls. He shook those overalls. He dragged them across the yard and got them dirty. Serena had to wash them all over again. So she didn't love Tough Enough so much.

Irby, the next oldest Tatum boy, loved Tough Enough until Tough Enough dug a hole under the pigpen. The pigs in the pen were Irby's pigs. Tough Enough wanted to get in and have a good visit with them.

When he finished digging, he backed out to scratch a sudden flea. Before he could squeeze into the hole again, seven little pigs squeezed out—one by one, push push push, grunt grunt grunt.

Tough Enough had a fine time chasing them. But Irby had a hard time finding them and catching them. So Irby didn't love Tough Enough so much.

Annie Mae, the youngest Tatum girl, loved Tough Enough until he chewed up the quilt she was piecing. After that she didn't love him so much. "Bad dog, bad dog, bad dog," she used to say to him.

Grandma Tatum and Grandpa Tatum loved Tough Enough until a little while after Grandma Tatum fried heaps and heaps of chicken for a great big family homecoming. Dozens and dozens of Beanie's kinfolk came. There were eleven aunts and fifteen uncles and thirty-one cousins and two other grandparents and seven great-aunts and five great-uncles.

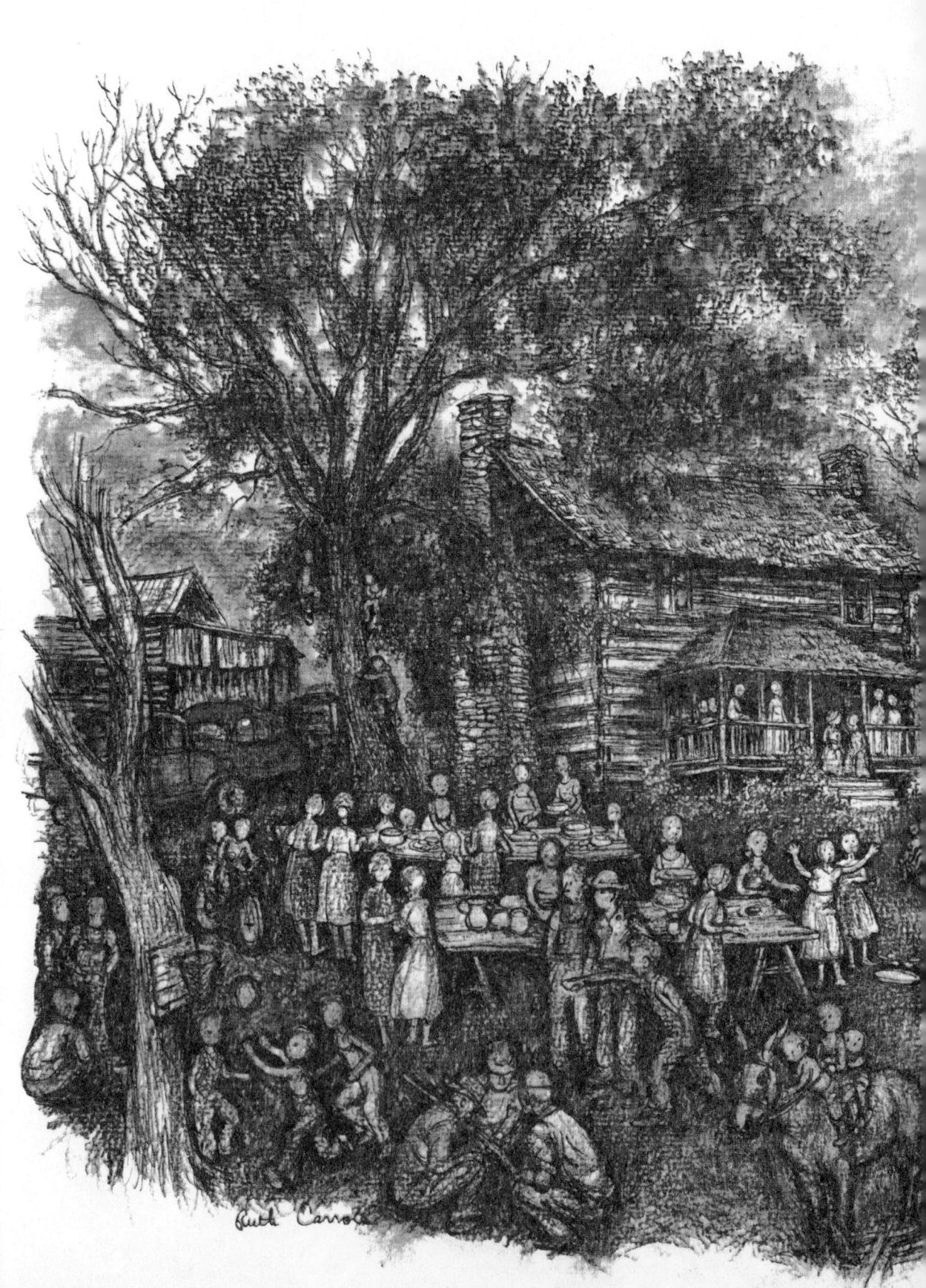

Tough Enough ran round and round, smelling the chicken smell. Then he rushed at the pile of chicken. He grabbed a big chicken breast, and he scattered a lot of chicken parts around. There were wings and breasts and drumsticks and second joints all over the place.

So Grandma Tatum didn't love Tough Enough so much. And neither did Grandpa Tatum. And neither did the eleven aunts and fifteen uncles and thirty-one cousins and two other grandparents and seven great-aunts and five great-uncles.

Beanie and His Dog

Beanie's teacher loved Tough Enough and some other boys and girls in his practicing a square dance. Tough too—he had followed the school bus school.

He rushed right into the middle of the dance. He ran to Beanie's feet and caught hold of a leg of his overalls and hung on.

Beanie tripped over him and fell down, ker-plop! Beanie's partner tripped over Beanie and fell down, ker-plop! And the other two children Beanie and his partner had been dancing with tripped over Beanie and his partner and fell down, ker-plop!

So Beanie's teacher didn't love Tough Enough so much.

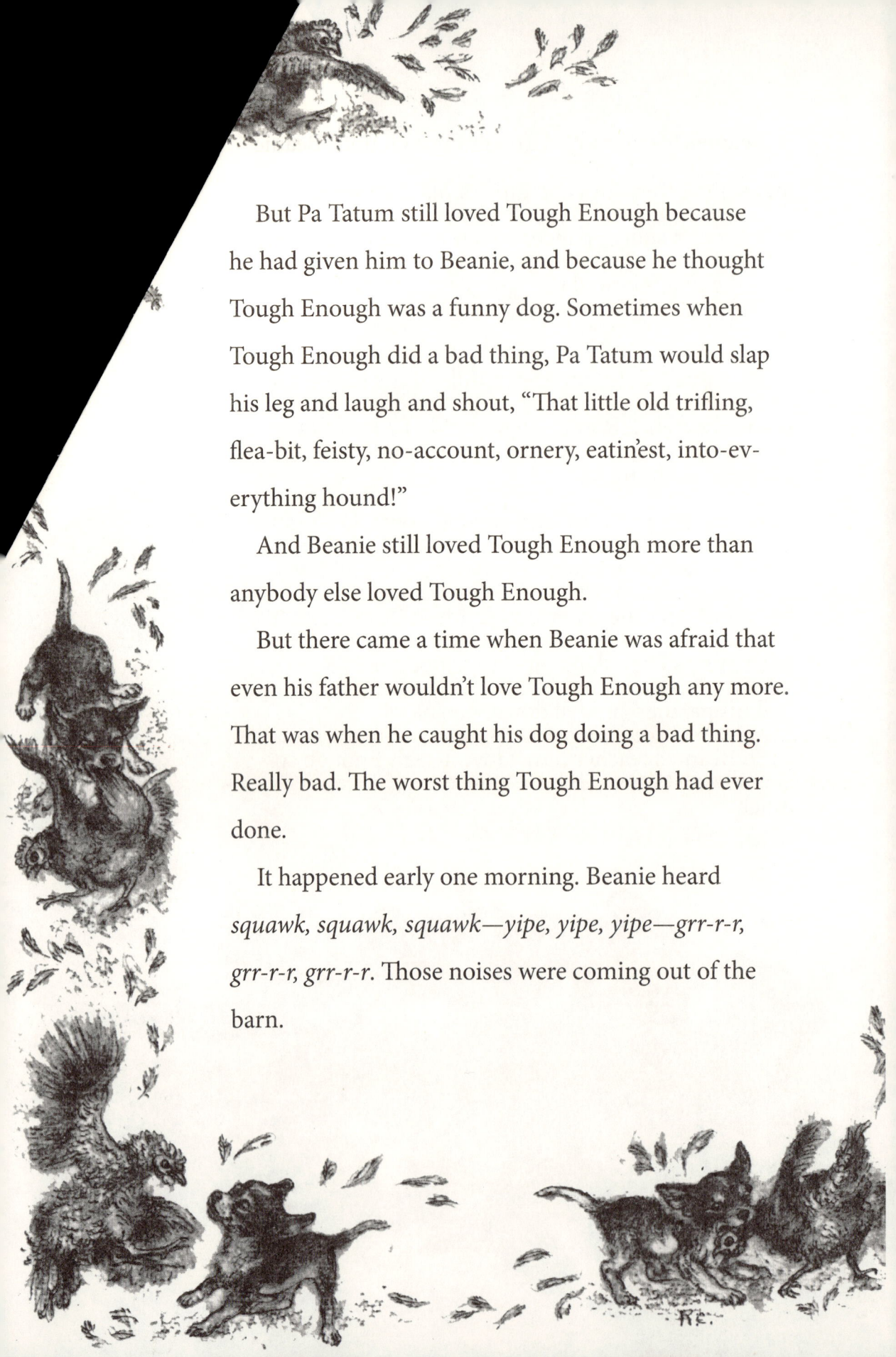

But Pa Tatum still loved Tough Enough because he had given him to Beanie, and because he thought Tough Enough was a funny dog. Sometimes when Tough Enough did a bad thing, Pa Tatum would slap his leg and laugh and shout, "That little old trifling, flea-bit, feisty, no-account, ornery, eatin'est, into-everything hound!"

And Beanie still loved Tough Enough more than anybody else loved Tough Enough.

But there came a time when Beanie was afraid that even his father wouldn't love Tough Enough any more. That was when he caught his dog doing a bad thing. Really bad. The worst thing Tough Enough had ever done.

It happened early one morning. Beanie heard *squawk, squawk, squawk—yipe, yipe, yipe—grr-r-r, grr-r-r, grr-r-r*. Those noises were coming out of the barn.

He hurried in. He was so surprised by what he saw that, for a moment, he just stood and looked.

Tough Enough was trying to pull a hen off her nest. She was Little Queen, Annie Mae's pet bantam hen. He had her by the tail feathers. He was tugging away in the middle of a small feather storm. Flap, flap, flap, she was flapping her wings. Peck, peck, peck, she pecked at him till he caught her by the neck.

He was still snarling and growling. But his snarls and his growls sounded strange and choked because his mouth was full of feathers and full of Little Queen's neck. And Little Queen's squawks were hardly squawks at all now. Tough Enough's jaws were not letting much squawking come out.

Beanie got over his surprise. He ran to his dog. He gave him a good hard spank.

Tough Enough let go of Little Queen. He ran away. At first his tail was down, but then he put it up and waved it around. His eyes were bright and quick with

mischief. He looked as if he knew he was bad but didn't feel sorry about it.

Little Queen's squawks had stopped. But she was clucking loudly because her feelings and her neck and her tail were hurt.

Just before she settled herself back on her nest, Beanie saw there were two eggs in there. Had Tough Enough tried to get at them so he could bite into them and suck them? Or did he want to eat up Little Queen?

Beanie wondered and worried.

He felt very sad, one day later in the week, when Annie Mae went to her mother in tears. She said Little Queen hadn't come at all when she was feeding the chickens. Beanie and a lot of the Tatums looked and looked for Little Queen. But nobody could find her.

Beanie didn't say anything to anybody. But, over and over, he said to himself, "Tough Enough maybe made a chicken dinner out of Little Queen."

Beanie didn't dare tell his father. He was afraid that, if he did tell him, his father might say they just couldn't keep a chicken-killing dog, so they'd have to get rid of him.

Beanie was still worrying when he was riding in the school bus on his way to school. The other boys and girls were talking and laughing and wiggling and calling back and forth to one another. But Beanie just sat silent. He felt too sad to laugh or talk, and he was thinking too hard. Should he tell his father what he had seen Tough Enough doing? That was what he was asking and asking himself.

Even when one of the boys called him a pouty old possum, he didn't show in any way that he had heard. He just stared straight ahead.

After the bus reached the school and Beanie and the others were in the classroom, Beanie was still

Beanie and His Dog

worrying. He couldn't keep his mind on his lesso[n.] was on Tough Enough and Little Queen.

When reading time came and he was reading aloud, he forgot his place. When it was arithmetic time and the teacher asked him, "What is twenty plus thirty?" he said, "Eleven." And when it was nature-study time and the teacher pointed to a picture of an American goldfinch hanging on the wall and asked, "Beanie, what bird is that?" Beanie said, "A banty hen."

All the boys and girls laughed and laughed and laughed.

After class the teacher said, "Whatever was the matter, Beanie?" But he just looked down at his feet and couldn't answer. There was a tight lump in his throat.

Pretty soon he got some words out past the lump. "Excuse me, ma'am," he said.

...pper, Pa Tatum said, "Annie Mae ... le banty hen is missing. It's Letty ... st be a varmint around, a varmint ... for hens. He's liking them more and

... nodded. "That critter could plumb eat us ... ns, and most likely he'll do it. If I got to quit eating fried chicken because there's no chickens left, I sure will miss fried chicken."

Beanie squirmed. He felt unhappy. Most of his unhappiness had gone to the bottom of his stomach.

Annie Mae said sadly, "Chicken and dumplings, that's what I like the best. I sure will miss chicken and dumplings."

"I sure will miss scrambled eggs," said Irby.

"I sure will miss egg custard pie," Buck said.

"And we won't have any sweet bread," wailed Annie Mae.

"Or any stacked cake," said Serena.

"Or any cake at all," said Ma Tatum.

"When you come right down to it," said Pa Tatum, "I'll miss eggs with ramps the worst. Eggs brisked up

so strong with spicy-like ramps, they're ready to jump off my plate."

Beanie had stopped eating. His mother looked at him. "Beanie, are you sick?" she asked gently.

"I'm just not hungry, Ma," he said in a small voice.

Pa Tatum tilted his cup and drank the last coffee drops. He stood up. His mouth looked hard and turned-down like a turtle's mouth.

He strode to the fireplace. He took down his gun and started oiling it.

Suddenly he said, "I'm going to get that critter. Sooner or later, I'll get him."

Beanie gave a jump, almost as if something had struck him. "I got to tell Pa right now," he said. But he said it to himself.

He took a deep breath and began, "Oh, Pa…"

"Yes, son?" his father asked.

But Beanie couldn't get out the words he had meant to say. He just said, "Wish spring would come. Looks like the ice won't ever melt. Looks like I won't ever

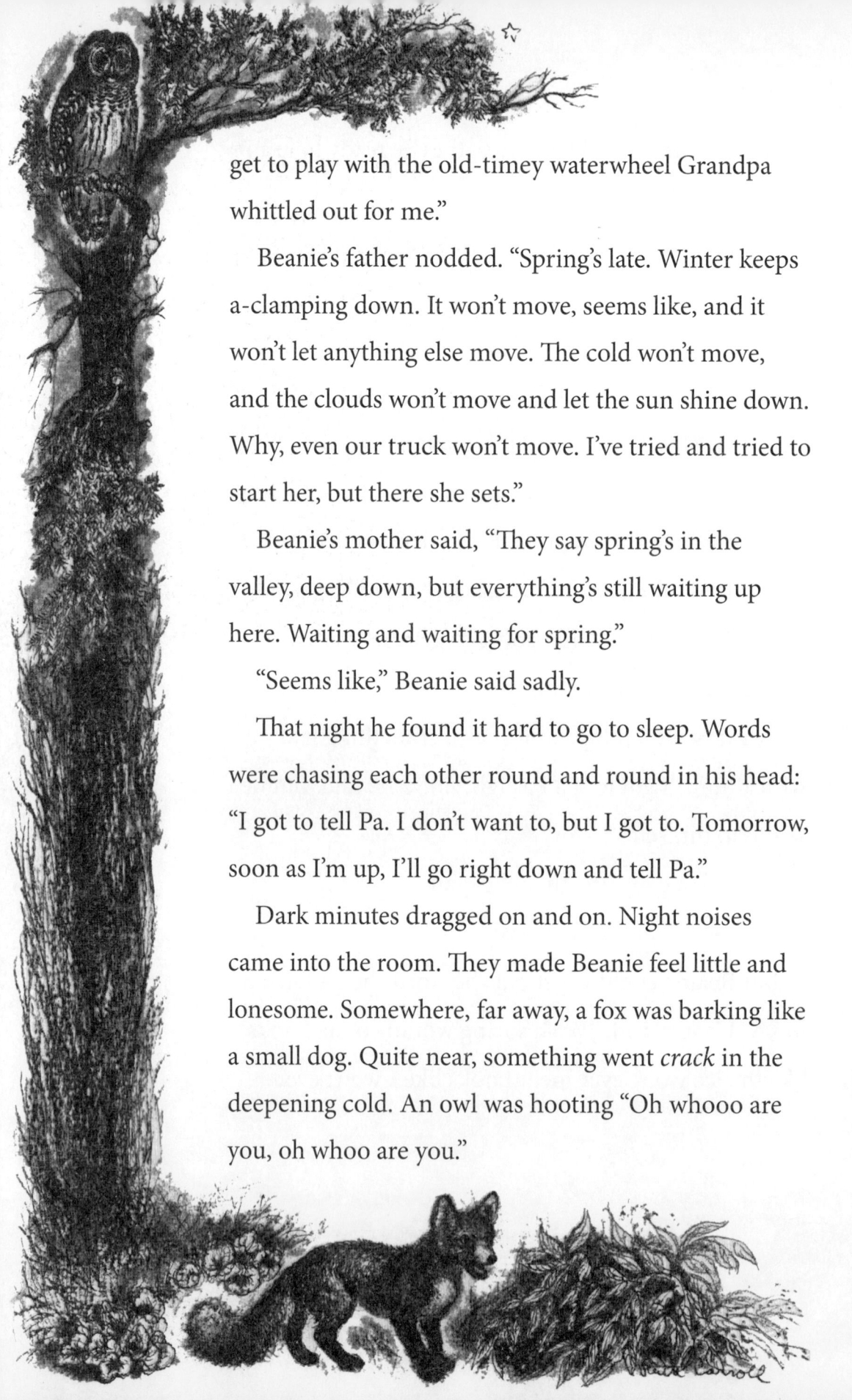

get to play with the old-timey waterwheel Grandpa whittled out for me."

Beanie's father nodded. "Spring's late. Winter keeps a-clamping down. It won't move, seems like, and it won't let anything else move. The cold won't move, and the clouds won't move and let the sun shine down. Why, even our truck won't move. I've tried and tried to start her, but there she sets."

Beanie's mother said, "They say spring's in the valley, deep down, but everything's still waiting up here. Waiting and waiting for spring."

"Seems like," Beanie said sadly.

That night he found it hard to go to sleep. Words were chasing each other round and round in his head: "I got to tell Pa. I don't want to, but I got to. Tomorrow, soon as I'm up, I'll go right down and tell Pa."

Dark minutes dragged on and on. Night noises came into the room. They made Beanie feel little and lonesome. Somewhere, far away, a fox was barking like a small dog. Quite near, something went *crack* in the deepening cold. An owl was hooting "Oh whooo are you, oh whoo are you."

Minutes turned into hours. Beanie dozed and wakened and dozed and wakened again. His open eyes saw the first faint light of day.

"Now it's tomorrow, and I got to tell Pa," he whispered over and over and over. But at last he stopped.

He was asleep.

Chapter Two

Voices wakened Beanie. His brothers, Buck and Irby, were getting up early, as usual, though it was Saturday. Before long they went clunking downstairs.

But Beanie still lay in bed. He was lonesome, but he couldn't make himself get up. He had never felt so lonesome in all his life. It was a sort of chilliness inside.

He heard a scratch-scratch-scratching coming up the stairs to the loft. Tough Enough came rushing in.

Beanie and His Dog

He jumped up on the bed and began to lick Beanie's face. That made the thought of getting up even harder to bear—the thought of telling his father what Tough Enough had done.

From below he heard a voice—his mother's. It was high and impatient. "Beanie! You come right down to breakfast this minute."

"I'm coming, Ma," he called back. But still he didn't get up.

Pretty soon he heard footsteps—his mother's steps coming up the stairs. He knew his mother would not want Tough Enough there on the bed. Quickly he tried to push his dog off, but he didn't push hard enough. The dog spread out all fours, bracing himself. Beanie pulled a quilt over him in a hurry.

Ma Tatum came in. She hurried to the bed. She put a hand on Beanie's forehead to see if he had a fever.

"Do you feel hot?" she asked.

He didn't answer. He couldn't, because he couldn't speak. He was pressing his lips together and holding

his breath, trying not to laugh. Tough Enough was tickling him, digging his nose into his ribs.

After a few tickling seconds, Beanie couldn't hold back any longer. His big breath burst out in a giggle. He shoved the dog away from him.

His mother whipped back the bedclothes. "Sakes alive!" she cried.

There lay Tough Enough himself in full view. He rolled over on his back. He stuck up his paws, and he stuck up his soft, fat stomach that was pink in places. He wiggled.

Beanie's mother caught him by the collar. "Bad dog, bad dog, *bad dog*," she said. She pulled him off the bed, and then she looked hard at Beanie.

"Beanie Tatum," she said, "you know that dog of yours isn't allowed in bed. I declare, you're as bad as he is. And now you get right up and dress and come down to breakfast. If you're well enough to laugh and carry on with that dog, you're well enough to eat breakfast."

Beanie dressed fast. He clunk, clunk, clunked downstairs, two steps at a time, and he jumped the last three steps and landed CLUNK on the floor.

The other Tatums were eating the last bites of their fried eggs. Beanie sat down at the table. His eyes went to his father's gun above the fireplace. Then he looked at the fried eggs on his plate. He didn't feel like eating them, but he got down three forkfuls.

After breakfast he went outdoors. He told himself he just couldn't put it off any longer. But he wondered if he could make himself tell.

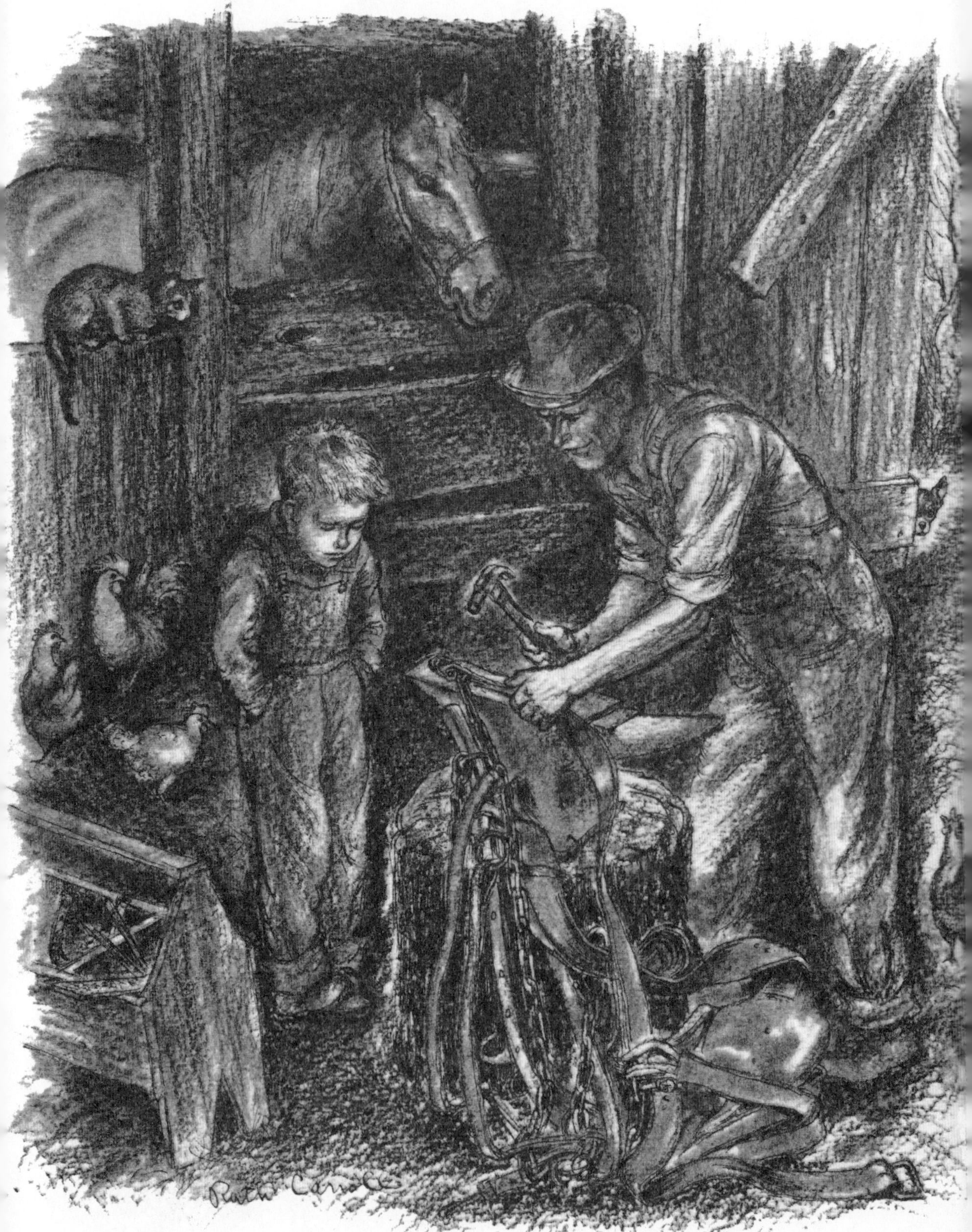

A chilly cloud, sitting on the mountain farm, was hiding things. Beanie shivered. His eyes strained through the fog as he picked his way along to the barn. Inside, he found his father mending a harness.

Beanie said, "Pa…"

His father looked up. "It's the beatin'est thing," he said, "how a harness wears so thin so fast."

There was a tight ache in Beanie's throat, but he tried again. "Yes, but Pa…"

"Wears all thin and frazzled," said his father, "long before it ought to."

"*Pa*," Beanie said, and his voice went high, "I got something to tell you. I don't want to, Pa, but I got to. It's about—Tough Enough."

His father put down the harness. "What is it, son?"

"Maybe—maybe Tough Enough ate up Little Queen and Letty Lou."

And then, at last, Beanie told all. When he had finished, his father didn't say a word, at first. He seemed to be thinking hard.

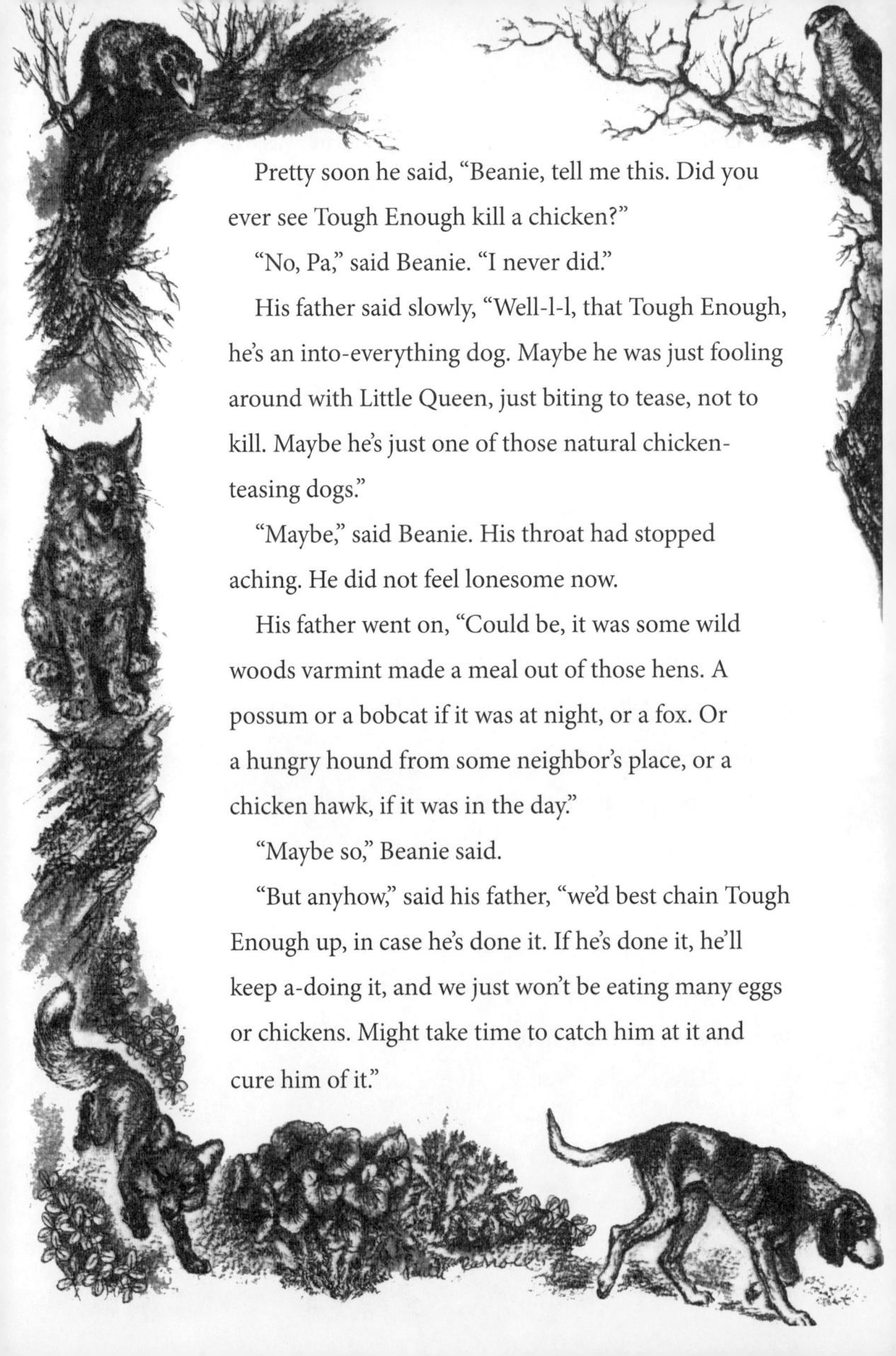

Pretty soon he said, "Beanie, tell me this. Did you ever see Tough Enough kill a chicken?"

"No, Pa," said Beanie. "I never did."

His father said slowly, "Well-l-l, that Tough Enough, he's an into-everything dog. Maybe he was just fooling around with Little Queen, just biting to tease, not to kill. Maybe he's just one of those natural chicken-teasing dogs."

"Maybe," said Beanie. His throat had stopped aching. He did not feel lonesome now.

His father went on, "Could be, it was some wild woods varmint made a meal out of those hens. A possum or a bobcat if it was at night, or a fox. Or a hungry hound from some neighbor's place, or a chicken hawk, if it was in the day."

"Maybe so," Beanie said.

"But anyhow," said his father, "we'd best chain Tough Enough up, in case he's done it. If he's done it, he'll keep a-doing it, and we just won't be eating many eggs or chickens. Might take time to catch him at it and cure him of it."

So Pa Tatum hunted and rummaged around for a chain. But the only chain he could find was a rusty one that snapped apart in his hands when he gave it a jerk.

He said, "Maybe that dog will keep raising a ruckus after he's chained up. Maybe there'll just be no living with him. Maybe it won't work out at all. But we'll try it, so here's what you do. Go down the Tatum Creek shortcut, down to the store in the deep valley, and buy a new chain."

"Yes, Pa," said Beanie, "and I'll take Tough Enough along. It'll maybe be his last chance to run loose."

Beanie went to his mother. He told her he was going down into the valley to buy a chain to chain up Tough Enough.

She nodded her head. "Annie Mae had better go, too, to keep an eye on you and that dog."

Beanie straightened his back and his neck and stood taller. He said, "*I'll* be the one that keeps an eye on them both."

"Well, good," said his mother. "Everybody will keep an eye on everybody else."

She began to put up a picnic lunch for Beanie and Annie Mae and Tough Enough. Beanie watched her do it. There was cornbread and ham and stacked cake for him and Annie Mae, and some scraps for Tough Enough.

Before the three started off, Pa Tatum said to Beanie and Annie Mae, "If I can start that ornery, half-froze truck, I'll pick you up at the store or when you're on your way home. If I can't get the truck a-going, you can hitch a ride back with one of the neighbors, most likely. Either way, you'll do all right."

Beanie put up his chin. "I'll manage things fine," he said.

Off he started. Annie Mae caught up with him, and Tough Enough went racing ahead through the mists that were lifting a little. Beanie had the lunch in a paper bag. His waterwheel was hanging from his belt, tied there with a piece of string.

They reached the place where Tatum Creek started. It came up in a deep bowl in the rocks. From ledges behind and above, Christmas ferns were hanging, and spongy green-brown mosses, and long melting icicles drip, drip, dripping.

Ruth Carroll

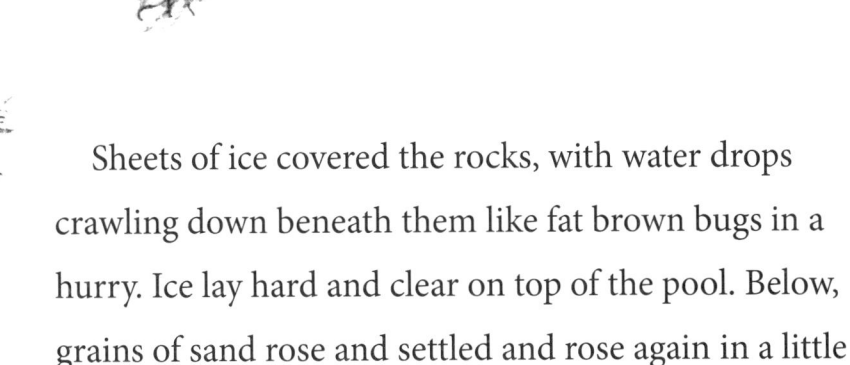

Sheets of ice covered the rocks, with water drops crawling down beneath them like fat brown bugs in a hurry. Ice lay hard and clear on top of the pool. Below, grains of sand rose and settled and rose again in a little up-and-down dance. That was where the water came spurting up out of the sand.

Tough Enough bit off an icicle. But then he began to bark, and it fell out of his mouth. He was pointing his nose at an old hemlock that the Tatums called the roosting tree. Chickens were still perching on its branches.

"Hey, Tough Enough!" Annie Mae called out. "You quit pestering those hens. Bad dog!"

Beanie said unhappily, "He's just telling them it's time to get up. It's still so dark and foggy, they don't know it's past break of day."

The three began to go down the trail that followed the tiny stream. Here the brook was just a ribbon of ice with a trickle of water flowing over dark leaves underneath.

"I like a talking creek," said Beanie. "I like to listen to it talk. But our creek's frozen up so hard on top, it can't say a word."

"Not a single little water word," said Annie Mae.

From time to time, Tough Enough's nose would bring him news. He would go barking and bounding off the trail on side trips of his own.

"He's feeling mighty frisky now," said Beanie. "He's feeling way, way up. But he's going to feel way, way down after he's chained."

"Yes," said Annie Mae, "just wait. We'll likely hear such tall howling, I reckon Ma and Pa just won't stand for it."

Beanie kicked a stone and sent it skittering.

"Beanie, you quit that," Annie Mae called out. "You'll scuff up your shoes."

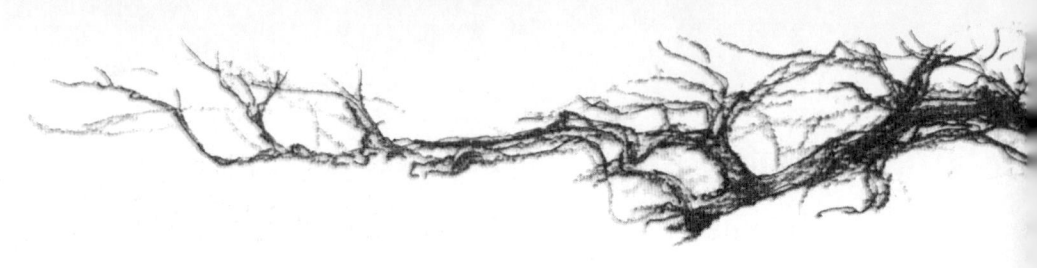

He didn't answer. His eyes were on a thing like a giant snake—the stem of a grapevine looping and twisting among the branches of oak trees. He leaped up. He caught a loop and swung back and forth, with Tough Enough barking below.

"Hey, Beanie!" called his sister. "Come down from there before you snag your britches."

"Look-a-here, Annie Mae," said Beanie, "you quit talking at me. Even if I am the youngest, you got no call to boss me."

Annie Mae said, "I'm not bossing you. Ma told me to keep an eye on you and that dog, and I'm doing it. Now you get down from there."

But Beanie didn't let go until he was tired of swinging.

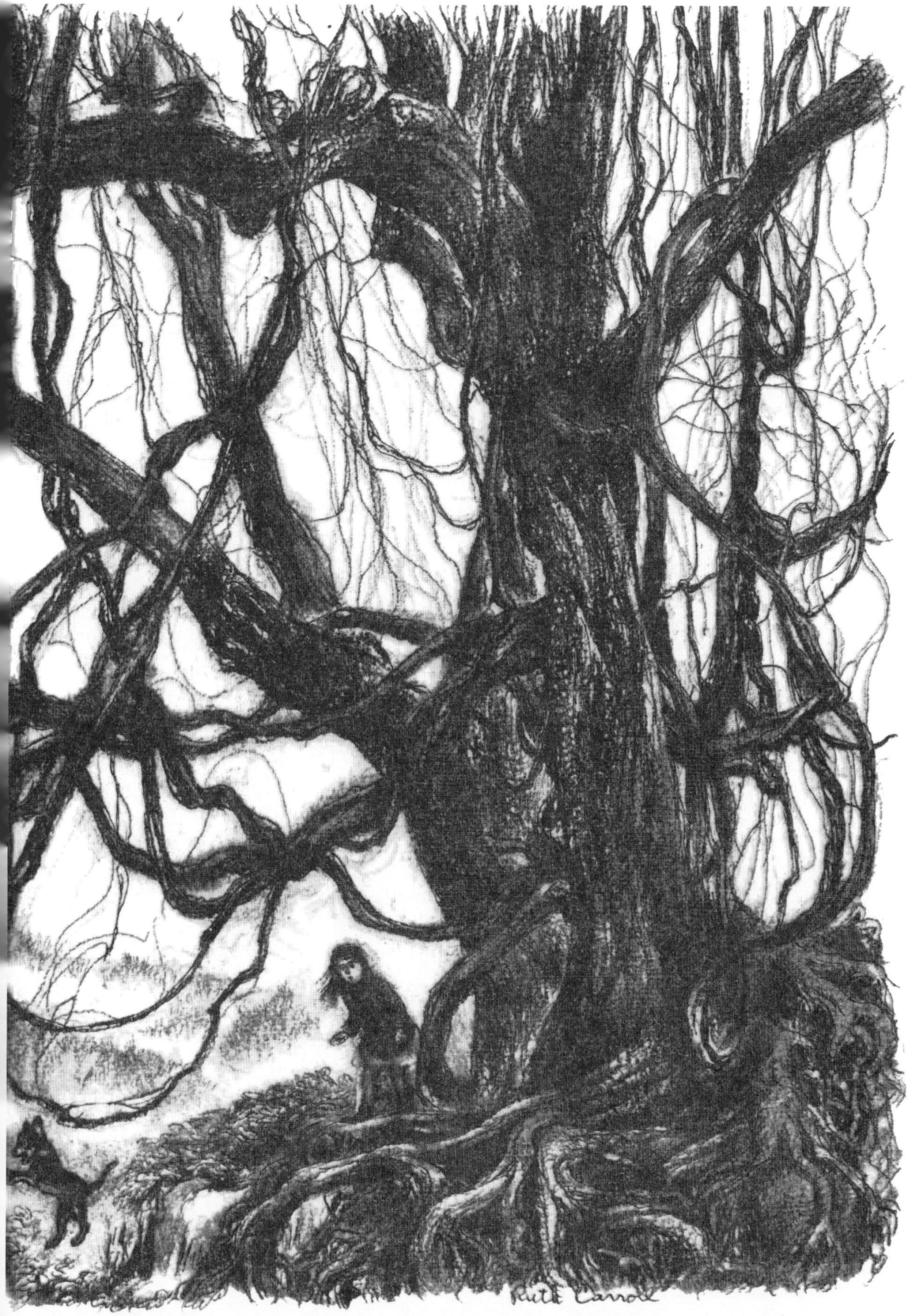
Ruth Carroll

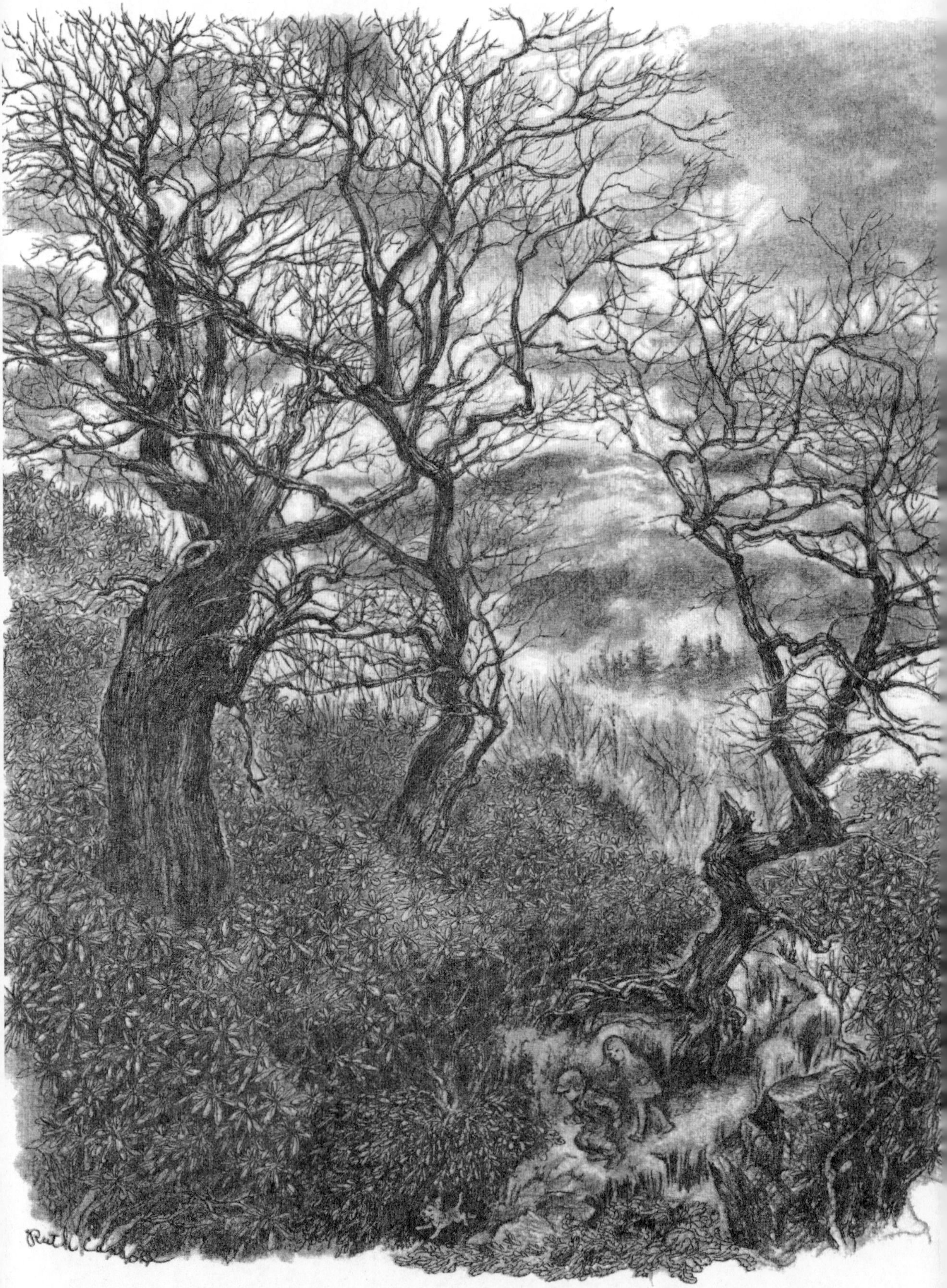

They went on down, on down, on down.

All of a sudden, Annie Mae said, "Listen! Do you hear something ahead?"

"Why, yes," said Beanie happily. "It sounds like—it sounds like our creek. Our creek's talking."

"Whispering, like," Annie Mae said.

"Whispering," said Beanie.

They went faster. Pretty soon they came to a place where all the water in the stream was flowing, flowing down.

Above, the high morning fog was thinning. The sun was burning it away. Then the sun itself came out, bright and strong. It drew sweet scents from brown hemlock needles and dead leaves.

Annie Mae and Beanie took off their winter jackets and tied them around their waists by the sleeves. Tough Enough's tongue was hanging out.

They went on down, on down, on down. Past the

yellow-browns and silver-grays of tree trunks, branches, twigs. Past the pale leaves still clinging to some trees. Through green laurel thickets and tangled dead briars.

And little by little, they found spring.

Spring was in the first flowers they saw—trailing arbutus blossoms hiding under shiny leaves. Annie Mae touched them with her nose, drawing in their fragrance.

Spring was in every bluet. It was in the bloodroot; it was in the hepatica; it was in the jack-in-the-pulpit. It was in a family of bird's foot violets shyly at home in a hollow in an old beech tree.

Spring was in the new fly that Tough Enough went *snap* at. It was in the red salamander he poked with his nose. It was in the tiny blue butterflies he chased off the trail.

It was in a spider warming himself on a rock.

Spring was in the foam flower farther down below. It was in the honey scent of service tree blossoms, in the orange-reds of bursting buckeye buds, in the russet haze of new maple leaves. It was in the painted trillium, in the wind flower, in the witch hobble. It was in the tufty blooms of little pussy-toes.

Spring was in the song of a white-throated sparrow, pure and sweet as a lonesome flute.

Spring was all around.

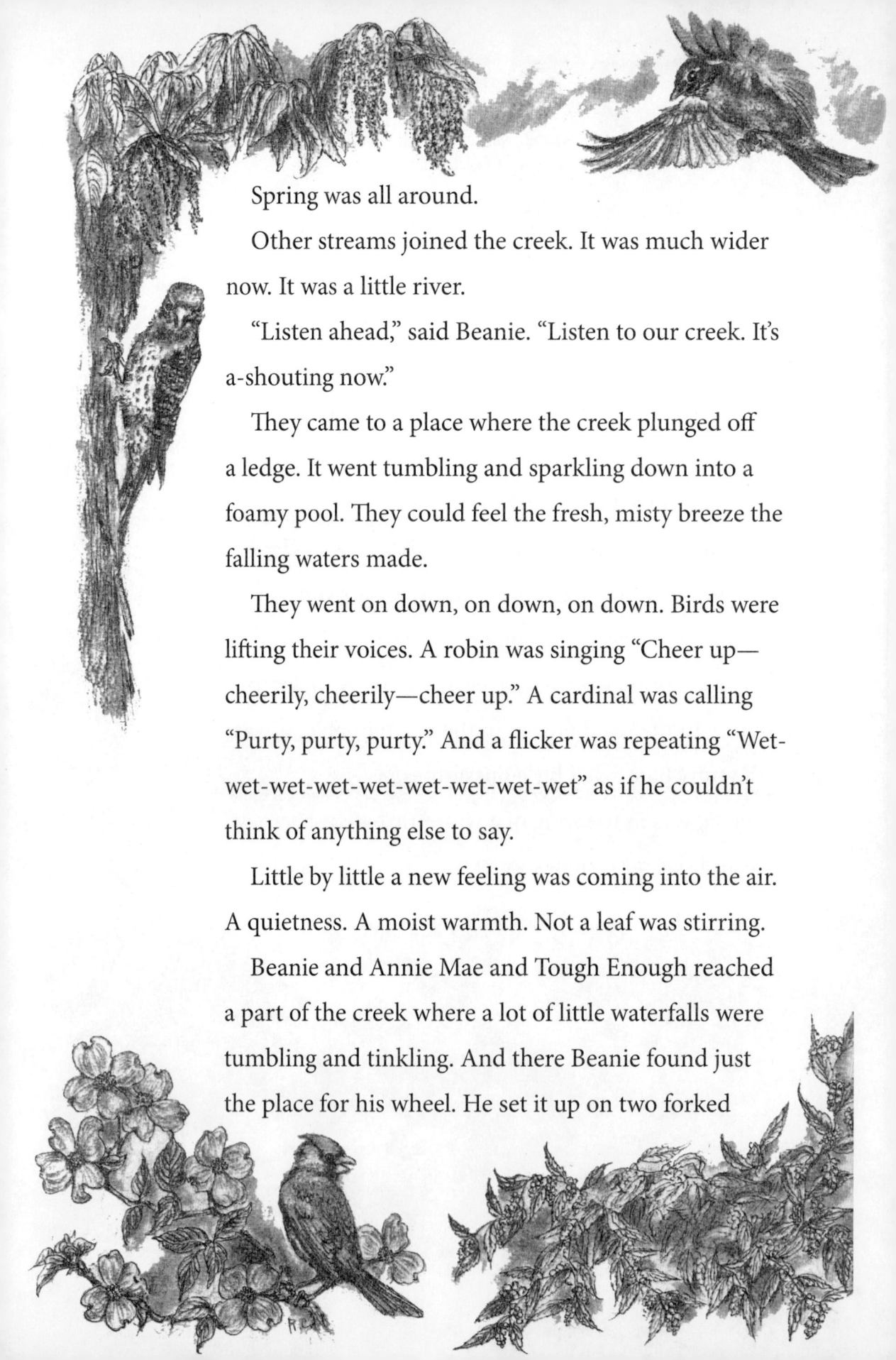

Other streams joined the creek. It was much wider now. It was a little river.

"Listen ahead," said Beanie. "Listen to our creek. It's a-shouting now."

They came to a place where the creek plunged off a ledge. It went tumbling and sparkling down into a foamy pool. They could feel the fresh, misty breeze the falling waters made.

They went on down, on down, on down. Birds were lifting their voices. A robin was singing "Cheer up—cheerily, cheerily—cheer up." A cardinal was calling "Purty, purty, purty." And a flicker was repeating "Wet-wet-wet-wet-wet-wet-wet-wet-wet" as if he couldn't think of anything else to say.

Little by little a new feeling was coming into the air. A quietness. A moist warmth. Not a leaf was stirring.

Beanie and Annie Mae and Tough Enough reached a part of the creek where a lot of little waterfalls were tumbling and tinkling. And there Beanie found just the place for his wheel. He set it up on two forked

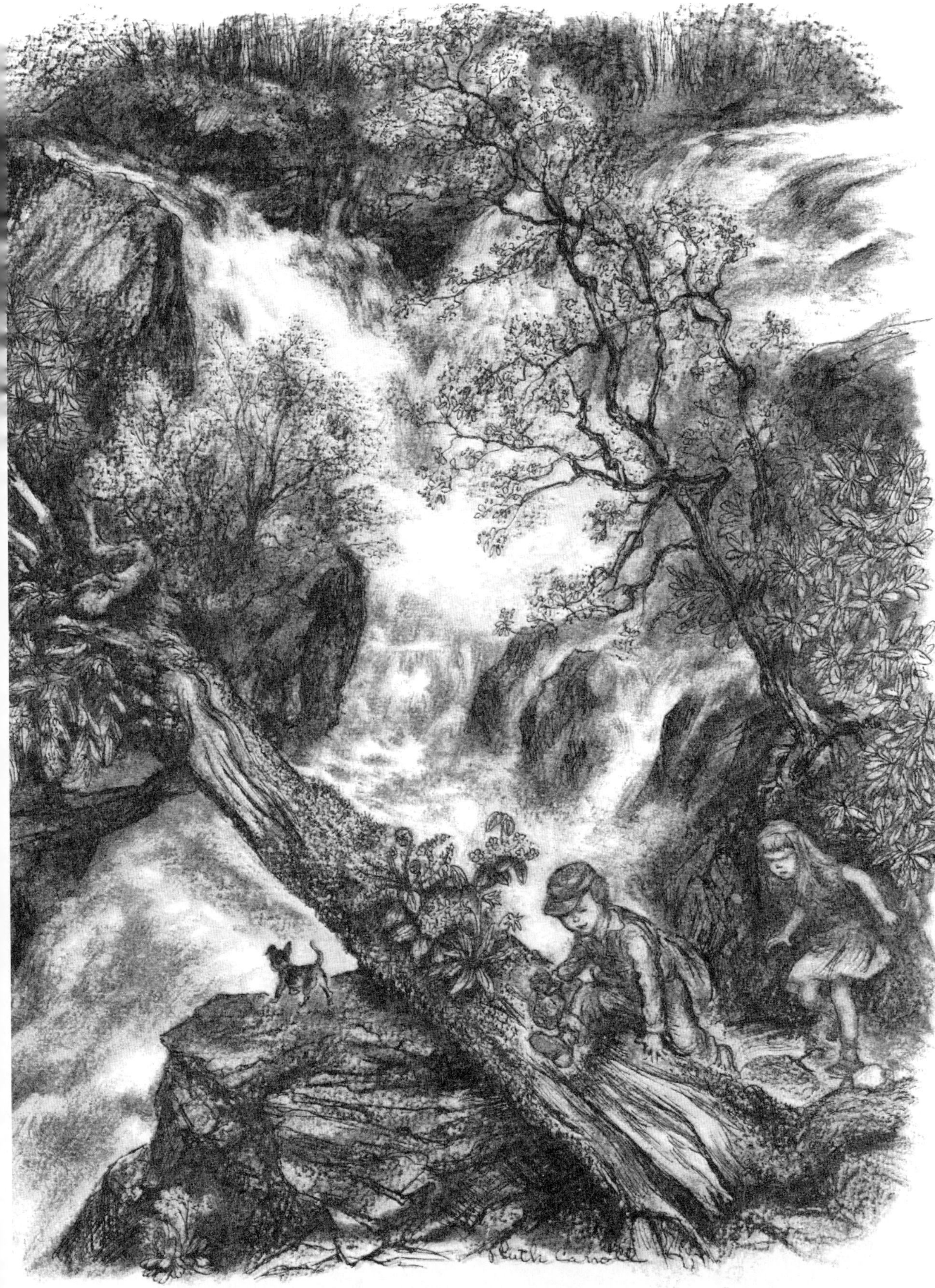

sticks so water would go pouring over it.

It began to turn.

"It's pretty," said Annie Mae. She made the word sound like "purty."

Beanie smiled. "It's the purtiest thing in the cove."

He gathered some twigs, and then he scooped up some of the best mud he could find. He made a little log mill-house, beside the turning wheel, out of the mud and the twigs.

His sister looked at him hard. "Beanie, I declare, there's mud all over you, pretty near."

Beanie said quickly, "Aw, it'll dry up and shake off. I'm hungry. Let's eat our lunch."

So Annie Mae opened the lunch bag. Tough Enough came wagging and barking in a begging way. The three ate their lunch.

Pretty soon Annie Mae stopped chewing. She looked all around and around.

"There isn't a whuff of air," she said. "Things are all scary-still."

"It's fixing to rain," Beanie said.

"Look-a-there!" said Annie Mae. "It's raining already, way back up the cove."

Beanie turned and looked. He saw huge purple-black clouds piled up and up and up. Gray curtains of rain were falling from them, hiding the mountains behind.

"It's bucketing down back there," he said. "It's a regular gully-washer, and it's heading our way!"

He picked up his waterwheel.

A brilliant tongue of lightning licked down. Then thunder came crashing and splitting. The mountains rolled and rolled and rolled the great sound back.

"Let's light out for the store!" cried Annie Mae.

Chapter Three

Beanie and Annie Mae hurried on down, on down, on down.

Suddenly the sun was gone. A chill, gusty wind began to blow. It pushed at the silver-bell trees and scattered their blossoms.

Annie Mae and Beanie put their jackets on.

"I felt a drop," said Annie Mae.

"*I* felt *two* drops," said Beanie. He and his sister and Tough Enough moved still faster down the trail. Lightning flashed and thunder boomed around them.

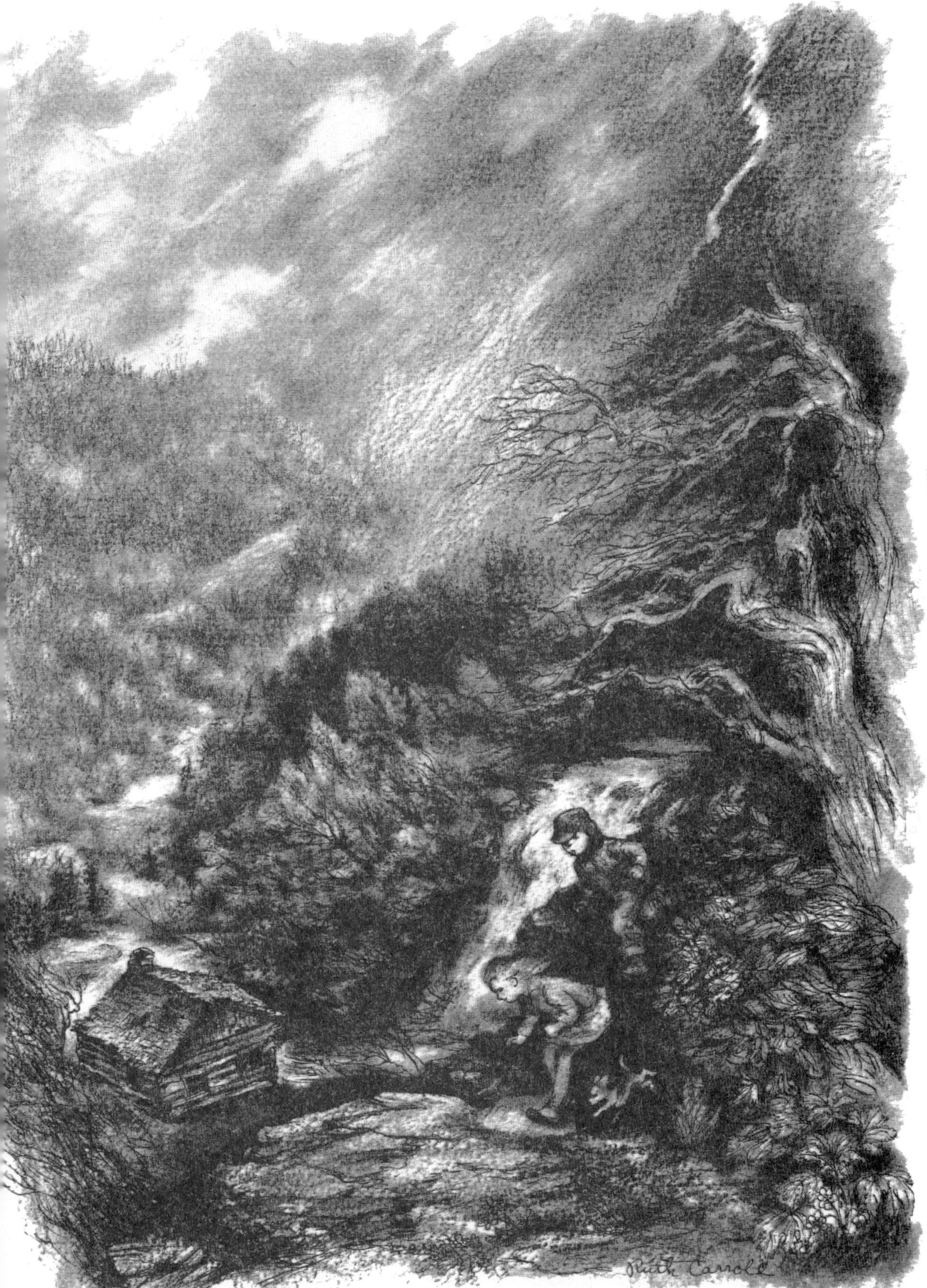
Ruth Carroll

Now they were in a narrow part of the cove, a part where the banks of the stream sloped up steeply. Ahead they saw an old cabin standing close to the creek.

More and more drops came driving until it was raining hard.

"We'll get plumb soaked," said Annie Mae, "if we don't wait out the storm in that empty old cabin yonder."

"Aw, we're not sugar," said Beanie. "A little rain won't melt us down."

"Beanie Tatum," said his sister, "you quit talking, you just run."

She led the way fast toward the cabin. Beanie made a face, but he followed.

The cabin door was hanging slightly open. Beanie shoved and it swung wide. The three ran in. He pushed the door tight shut.

"Whew!" said Annie Mae. She brushed a cobweb from her forehead. "We're lucky we're in here."

She and Beanie looked around in the light that seeped through a dirty, broken window pane. Tough

Enough was exploring with his nose.

There was nothing in the room except bits of glass. The thing Beanie noticed most was noise—the long boom-boom-booming of thunder, the wind tearing at branches overhead, the rain on the roof like the beating of drums, thousands of little drums. Already the roof was leaking in three places.

The drumming grew louder, faster. Outside the window, the cloudburst hid the view.

"Lands alive!" cried Beanie, "I feel like we're deep under water!"

Tough Enough finished his sniffing. He stood still. His large, intelligent ears were up. He seemed to be listening alertly, listening to sounds outside the cabin. He whimpered.

Slowly at first, then faster and faster, he started to run from wall to wall like a wild thing in a cage. He was barking now.

Beanie had never heard him bark in such a strange way. The noises came shrilling out of his throat as if they were hurting him. His eyes looked restless and unhappy. He seemed like a different dog.

"What's the matter with him?" Annie Mae called out. "He's acting crazy-like."

Tough Enough came running toward Beanie. He was trembling. He seized a leg of Beanie's trousers and tried to pull Beanie toward the door. Then he let go and jumped up on Annie Mae. His jaws closed on the edge of her skirt. He held on, tugging and tugging.

She jerked her skirt out of his mouth. "Bad dog," she cried, "*bad dog!*"

Tough Enough rushed to the door. He scratched and he scratched and he scratched on it. He looked back with begging eyes. He whined and whined and whined. His big, worried ears were up and quivering a little.

Beanie said, "He's acting like he's wild to get out and wild to get *us* out. Looks like his ears are telling him things, and he's trying to tell them to us. I'm going to open that door and see why he's all in a swivet."

"Don't you dare open that door!" Annie Mae screamed at him. "All the wind and rain in the world are waiting to come in. That dog's a crazy killer-dog.

Don't you pay him any mind. He's not worth a worm a robin's got a-hold of."

"He is *too* worth a worm!" Beanie said hotly.

Beanie put out a hand to pull the door open just as Annie Mae pressed both hands against it to hold it shut. For a few moments they struggled, Beanie pulling on the handle, Annie Mae pushing. Both were working hard, but the door didn't budge. It stayed shut.

Tough Enough was scratching at it more desperately than ever, and jumping and jumping and jumping up against it.

Suddenly, with all his strength, Beanie gave the handle an inward jerk. The door swung partly open.

Out darted Tough Enough. He turned, and he looked back, and he barked in a "Follow me!" way. Beanie squeezed out into the driving downpour.

For a second or two he just stood staring and listening. He didn't call out. He couldn't.

His eyes were on the creek. His ears were full of its rushing and its roaring.

It did not look or sound like the creek he knew. It was rolling its high waters right up to the cabin steps. Swirling and foaming, yellow-red with mud, it was sweeping along dead leaves and dead wood and the torn-away branches of trees. Second by second it was rising. Beanie could see it reaching up.

He got back his voice. "Come out!" he shouted. "Annie Mae, come out! The creek's gone wild. It's going to flood the cabin."

She came running. Beanie caught her hand.

Up behind the cabin, up in a laurel thicket above a steep bank, Tough Enough was barking loud "Come here!" barks.

Beanie and Annie Mae splashed through water up to their knees as they ran around a corner of the cabin. They started to climb the clay slope behind it, the bank directly under Tough Enough.

Wet leaves and stones kept sliding under their feet. Again and again they stumbled and slipped back. Whenever they could, they pulled themselves up by grasping small tree trunks and branches.

There came a snapping sound. "Oh!" screamed Annie Mae. A branch had broken. She was sliding toward deep water swirling at the bottom of the slope.

Beanie reached down. He clutched her jacket. Pulling, tugging, sometimes slipping, he drew her up.

They struggled into the thicket. Close to its outer edge, where the bushes grew thin, they rested.

Tough Enough was there. He threw himself on them, yelping, wiggling all over. He licked their faces; he licked their hands; he licked as much of their necks as he could lick.

Annie Mae and Beanie were panting. They lay on their stomachs, looking down at the flood. The cabin was half under water now.

They saw an uprooted tree come driving down in the current. End on, it struck the cabin with a muffled thud. And suddenly there wasn't any cabin. There was

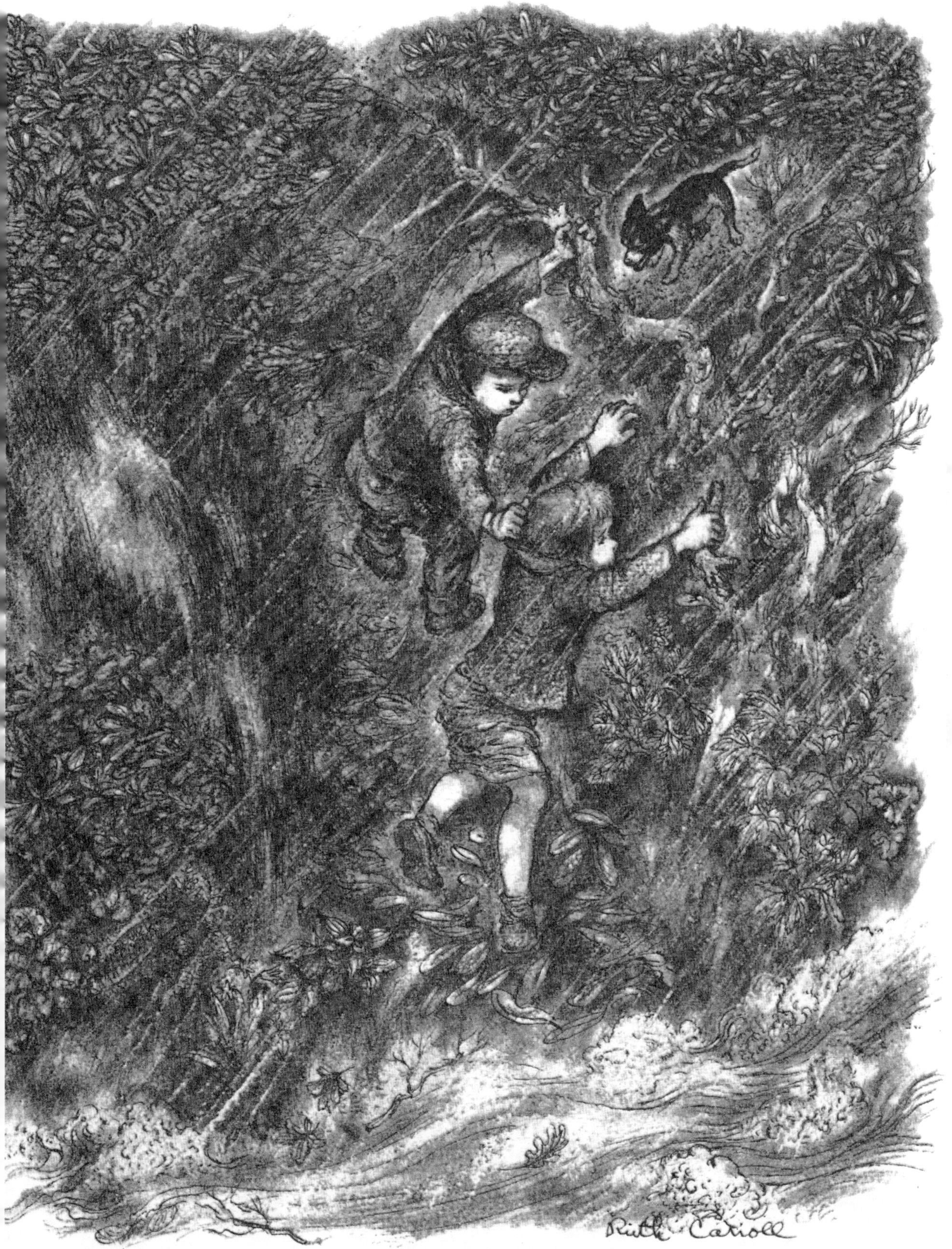
Ruth Carroll

nothing but logs and boards and shingles swirling downstream.

"Mercy on us!" cried Annie Mae.

Beanie caught hold of Tough Enough. He hugged him. He said, "You're just about the smartest little old dog there is."

Annie Mae petted and patted and petted Tough Enough. "If it wasn't for you—" she said to him. "If it wasn't—for you…" She looked at the rushing waters, at the place where the cabin had stood.

The rolling of thunder had stopped. The rain was slackening.

Annie Mae stood up. When she spoke again, her voice was sad. "It's easy walking now, to the road the store sets on. We'd best get going."

Off again the three started. Beanie wasn't hurrying. His feet didn't want to move. He and Annie Mae and Tough Enough reached the rutty road too soon for him.

Rain was still falling. It was running down out of Beanie's and Annie Mae's hair. It dripped from their noses and their chins; it squished and it squinched in their shoes. It was giving Tough Enough's coat a glued-down look.

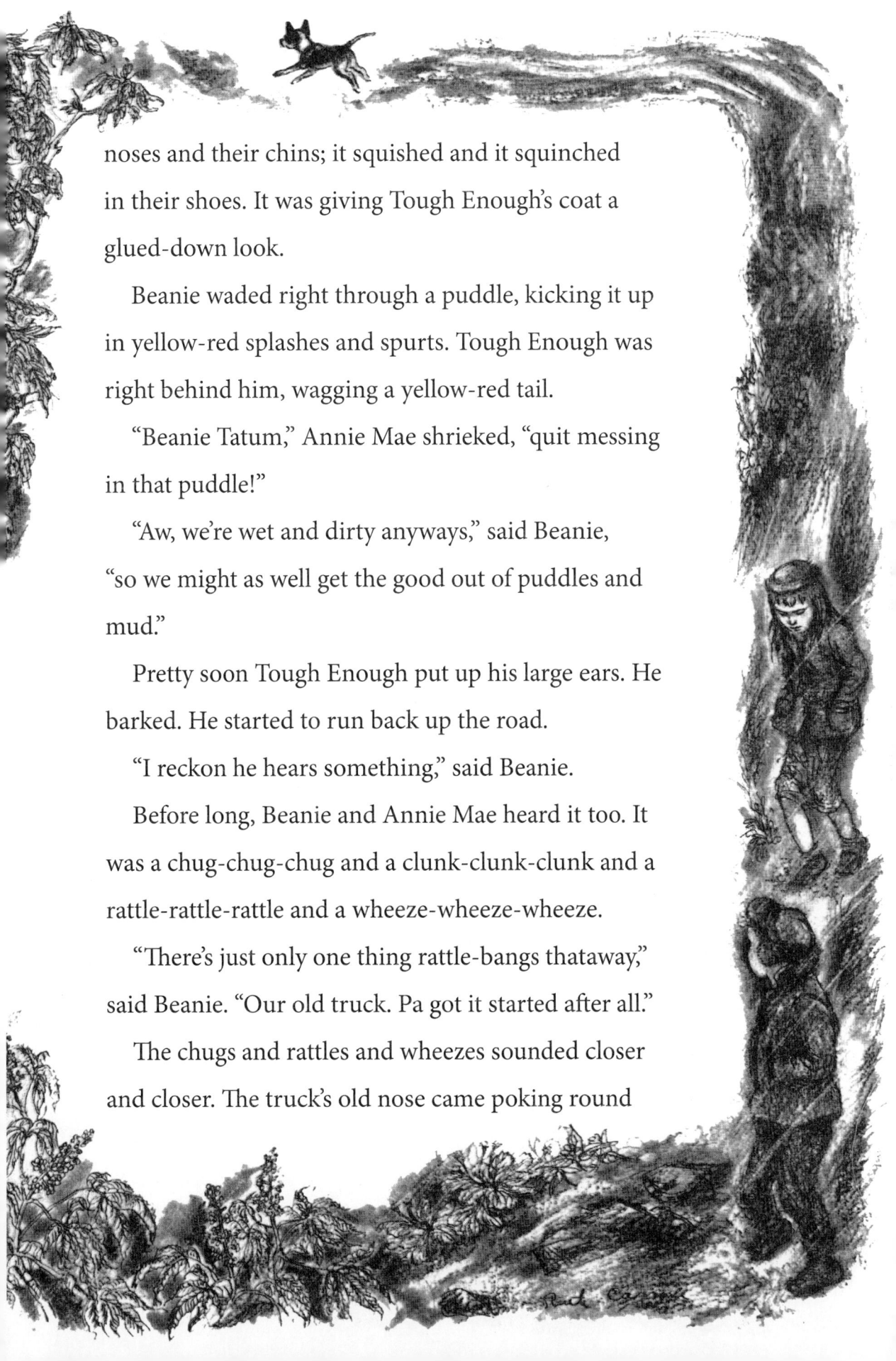

Beanie waded right through a puddle, kicking it up in yellow-red splashes and spurts. Tough Enough was right behind him, wagging a yellow-red tail.

"Beanie Tatum," Annie Mae shrieked, "quit messing in that puddle!"

"Aw, we're wet and dirty anyways," said Beanie, "so we might as well get the good out of puddles and mud."

Pretty soon Tough Enough put up his large ears. He barked. He started to run back up the road.

"I reckon he hears something," said Beanie.

Before long, Beanie and Annie Mae heard it too. It was a chug-chug-chug and a clunk-clunk-clunk and a rattle-rattle-rattle and a wheeze-wheeze-wheeze.

"There's just only one thing rattle-bangs thataway," said Beanie. "Our old truck. Pa got it started after all."

The chugs and rattles and wheezes sounded closer and closer. The truck's old nose came poking round a bend. Tough Enough was running along beside it, barking and barking away.

"Look-a-there," cried Annie Mae, "who all's in the truck!"

Pa Tatum and Ma Tatum and Buck and Serena and Irby were all squeezed together in the front seat.

"Hey!" Pa Tatum called out to Annie Mae and Beanie. His whole face was a grin. "We been worried up about you. Bad flood. Tore things up and flattened 'em down."

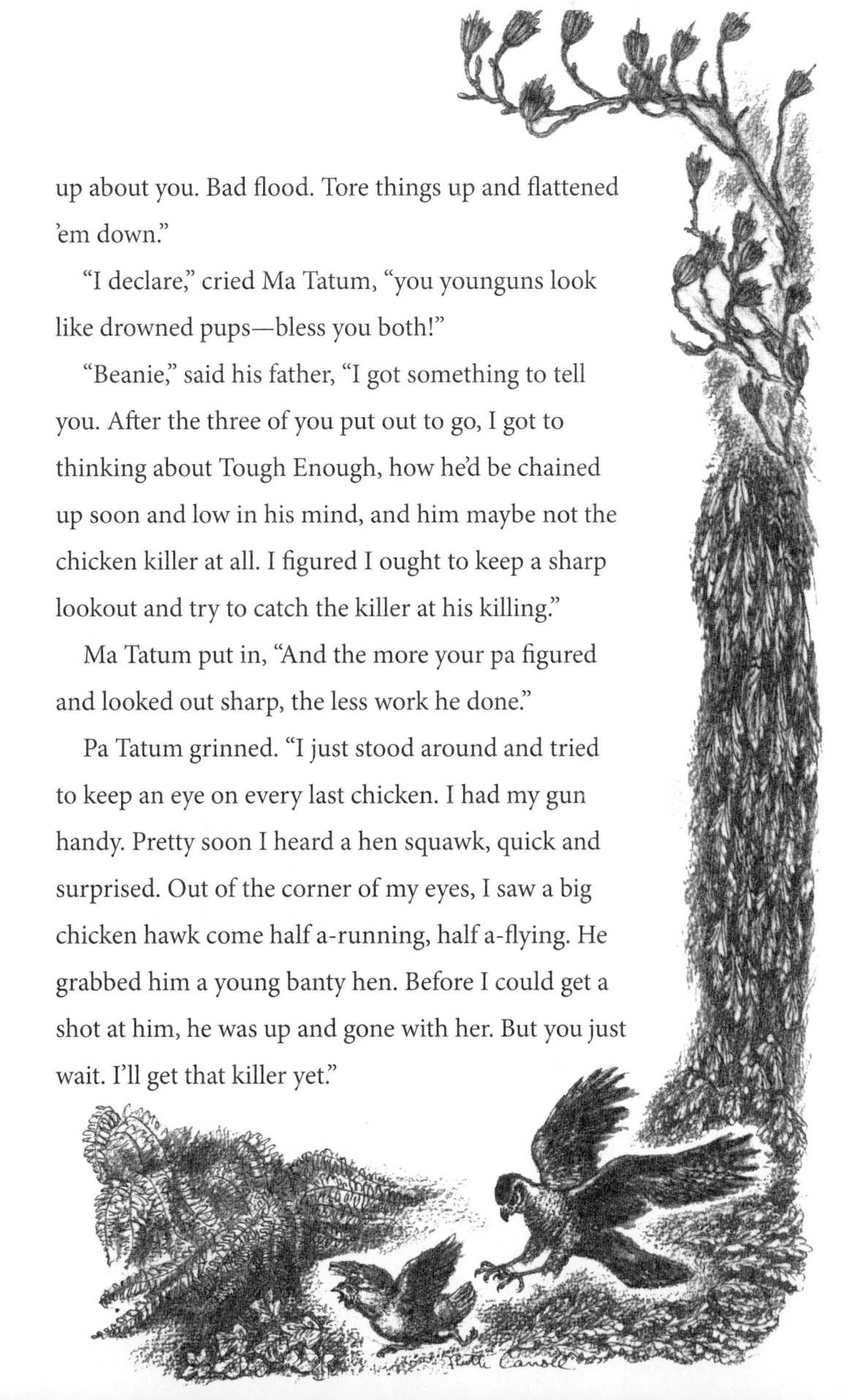

"I declare," cried Ma Tatum, "you younguns look like drowned pups—bless you both!"

"Beanie," said his father, "I got something to tell you. After the three of you put out to go, I got to thinking about Tough Enough, how he'd be chained up soon and low in his mind, and him maybe not the chicken killer at all. I figured I ought to keep a sharp lookout and try to catch the killer at his killing."

Ma Tatum put in, "And the more your pa figured and looked out sharp, the less work he done."

Pa Tatum grinned. "I just stood around and tried to keep an eye on every last chicken. I had my gun handy. Pretty soon I heard a hen squawk, quick and surprised. Out of the corner of my eyes, I saw a big chicken hawk come half a-running, half a-flying. He grabbed him a young banty hen. Before I could get a shot at him, he was up and gone with her. But you just wait. I'll get that killer yet."

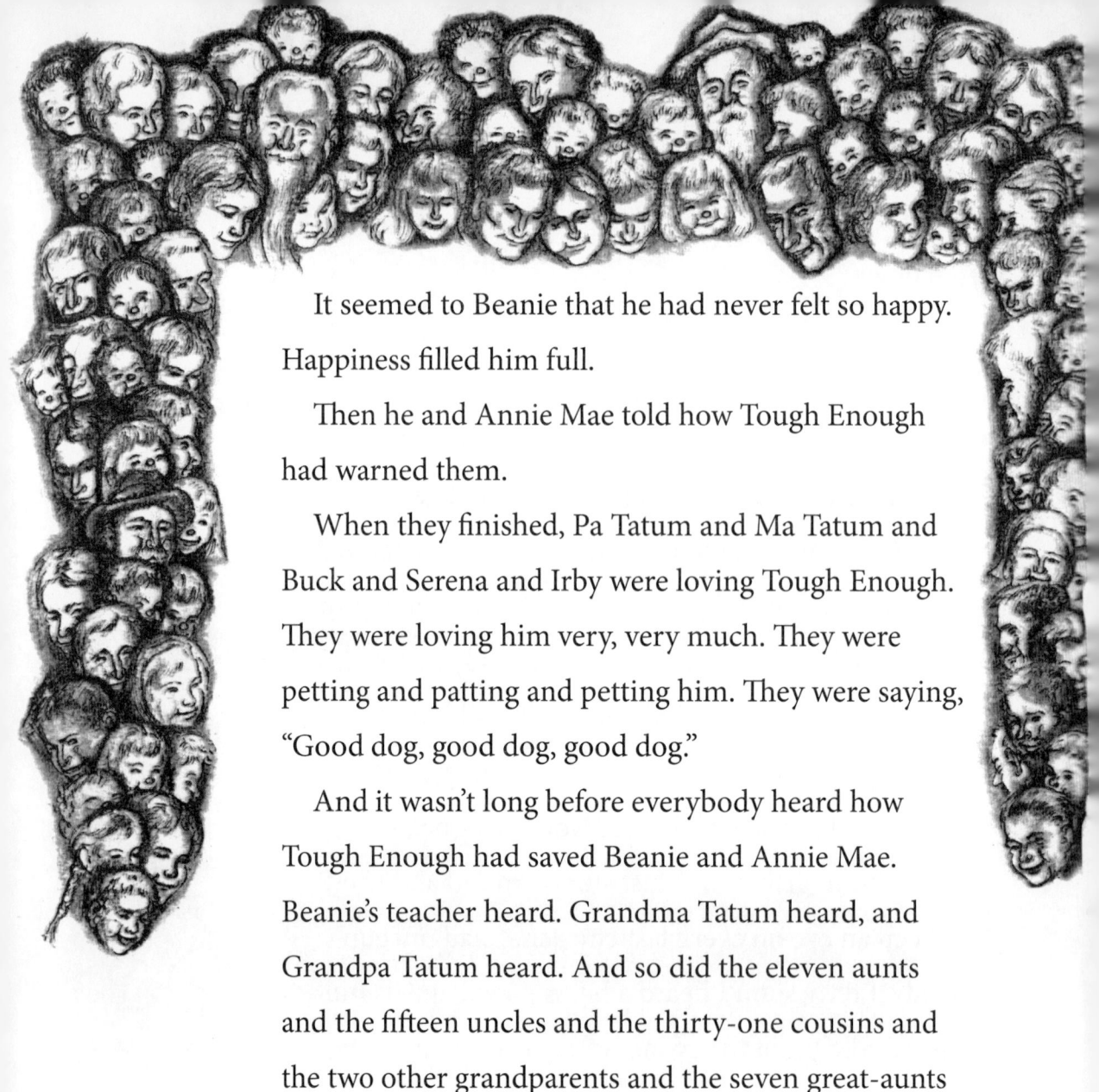

It seemed to Beanie that he had never felt so happy. Happiness filled him full.

Then he and Annie Mae told how Tough Enough had warned them.

When they finished, Pa Tatum and Ma Tatum and Buck and Serena and Irby were loving Tough Enough. They were loving him very, very much. They were petting and patting and petting him. They were saying, "Good dog, good dog, good dog."

And it wasn't long before everybody heard how Tough Enough had saved Beanie and Annie Mae. Beanie's teacher heard. Grandma Tatum heard, and Grandpa Tatum heard. And so did the eleven aunts and the fifteen uncles and the thirty-one cousins and the two other grandparents and the seven great-aunts and the five great-uncles.

So they all loved Tough Enough very, very much. "Good dog, good dog, good dog," they said.

But Beanie said a better thing: "That little old Tough Enough, he's the best dog in the world, I reckon."

More Books from The Good and the Beautiful Library!

Susie and Lizzie Boxed Set
by May Justus

Over the Hills to Nugget
by Aileen Fisher

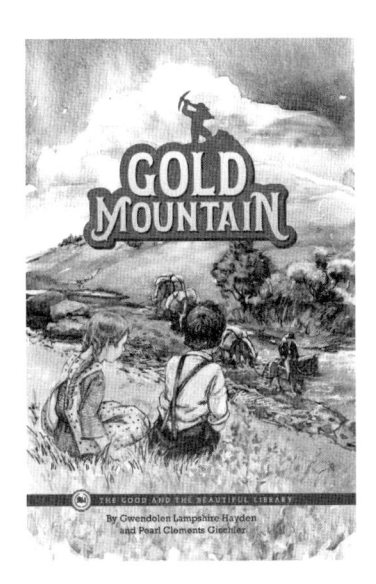

Gold Mountain
by Gwendolen Lampshire Hayden and Pearl Clements Gischler

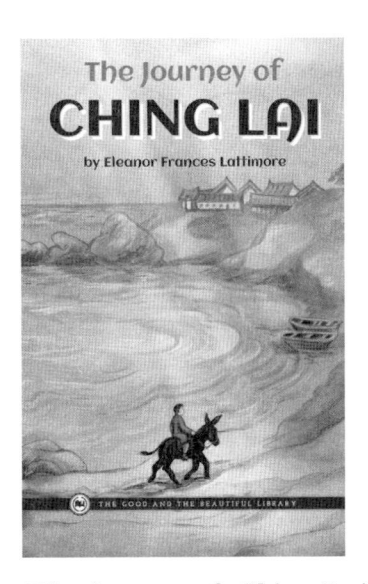

The Journey of Ching Lai
by Eleanor Frances Lattimore